# THE LANDING
## A NIGHT OF BIRDS

# THE LANDING

## A NIGHT OF BIRDS

ILLUSTRATED BY DAVID WONG

# KATHERINE SCHOLES

DOUBLEDAY

NEW YORK · LONDON · TORONTO · SYDNEY · AUCKLAND

The author wishes to acknowledge the assistance of Roger Scholes, Paul Schutze, and Bob Tomkins.

Published by Doubleday, a division of Bantam Doubleday Dell Publishing Group, Inc., 666 Fifth Avenue, New York, New York 10103

**Doubleday** and the portrayal of an anchor with a dolphin are trademarks of Doubleday, a division of Bantam Doubleday Dell Publishing Group, Inc.

First published in Australia 1987
by Hill of Content Publishing Company Pty. Ltd.
86 Bourke Street, Melbourne, Australia 3000

Designed by Diane Stevenson / SNAP•HAUS GRAPHICS

Library of Congress Cataloging-in-Publication Data

Scholes, Katherine.
The landing: a night of birds.

Summary: One stormy night at her grandfather's place on the windswept coast, Annie enters a boathouse occupied by injured sea birds and finds herself able to understand their speech.
[1. Birds—Fiction.   2. Fantasy]   I. Wong, David, ill.
II. Title.
PZ7.S3683Lan   1989   [Fic]   88-30953
ISBN 0-385-26191-8

*F*or Elizabeth and Robin,
who told me my first stories

# CHAPTER

# 1

HAIL BEAT DOWN INTO PEAKS AND TROUGHS OF BLACK WATER. Fish skulked far beneath the rolling swell, and the night sky was a cold and lonely place.

The first lightning streaked from cloud to cloud and cloud to sea—a double flash. It lit the foam-edged waves and then, for a moment, a white shape that hurled along in the wind. There was thunder, long and low, then more lightning—and the picture was caught again: long, tapering wings; a rosy-yellow beak; a dark eye.

Each great wing was as long as any man is tall. But in this wild wind the bird was tossed along like a paper plane—struggling over long mounds, bumps and heaps of troubled air. It flew with its head sunk low and eyes half closed against the beating hail. From the smooth, white undercarriage, a leg stuck down—a snag in the wind. And just above the webbed foot was a big, angry swelling; a half-healed wound.

The bird was tired.

There had been two days and three nights of this struggle with the storm—this endless, deadly game of trying to stay in the air with the least amount of effort. Moving just the end of a wing, if possible, or fanning out a few flight feathers— but sometimes making big, desperate movements, wrenching muscles.

Always working with the wind. Straining eyes during long nights of watching the waves ahead—judging by the rise and fall of big swells what to expect in the air above. Turning across the path of the wind to catch a rising current. Soaring upward, with careful trimming of the wings—and then, at last, a kind of cautious rest on the long glide down. Easing tired flight muscles, catching breath. Time to feel the cold edge of hunger, to search the waves for the silver flash of a stray fish jumping, or something floating dead. Coming to the end of the glide, opening the beak to sip the salt spray lifting from the waves. Gaining speed for the final drop, and at the last moment jamming the tail up to one side and lifting the outside wing—to turn fast into the wind. Then stretching wings for instant lift, up and up again.

For two days and three nights the bird had carved a path through the storm. Climbing and gliding, up and down— always ready to be thrown suddenly skyward in an updraft or snatched sideways then hurled toward the sea.

Wing joints ached, and sharp pains shot through almost every muscle. The injured leg throbbed, and burned in the cold air. It slowed down one side as it dragged in the wind, breaking the even balance of the wings. The rest of the streamlined body had to correct for it all the time, over-working one wing.

The bird was tired.

But there was no place to hide from the storm—no shelter from the heaving waves and fierce winds. So on and on the white bird flew, into the violent dark.

# CHAPTER

# 2

A SOUTHEASTERLY GALE SWEPT IN FROM THE COAST. IT BENT THE trees and made small waves in the river. It tore at the sides of the old boathouse and whistled through splintery gaps in its high timber walls.

It was early dawn. At a window of the boat builder's cottage a face appeared, and quickly pressed against the glass—pale in the early light.

Annie stared out. The sky was strangely clear.

There were birds all over the boatyard.

They were scattered among the salvaged rudders, sections of keel and heaps of coiled rope—in old boxes and crab pots; between oil drums and piles of wood.

There were four or five inside the old barbecue, several more in the lee of an upturned wheelbarrow—and even one sticking out of an old gumboot that lay on its side. From the landing stage by the river, right across the yard, to the cottage built up against the boathouse, the dark, gray birds filled every place of shelter.

And others lay out in the open, with ragged feathers, and limp wings flapping in the gale. They lay in the path of the winds as if they had fallen there and not moved. The storm light down on the landing stage cast a yellow haze into the gray morning, and touched their dark feathers with gold.

Annie raced down the hall and struggled with the door of Old Joe's bedroom. As usual it had gathered up the mat as it opened, and stuck fast, only slightly ajar. Annie could see him lying asleep, a woolen hat on his head, the cat curled up on his feet.

"Grandad?" she called loudly.

"Wha . . ." he answered without waking up.

Annie kicked at the door.

"WAKE UP!" she yelled.

The cat leaped up. It ran in panic across Old Joe's legs and up over his stomach, then clawed its way into the bed.

"Aaaaagh!" Old Joe shot up, suddenly fully awake. "What the heck? . . . Annie, I've told you—"

"Grandad," Annie interrupted urgently. "Outside . . ."

"Blasted cat," Old Joe groped among the bedclothes. "Where are ya?"

"THE YARD'S FULL OF BIRDS."

For a few moments Old Joe stared, blinking—caught by the look on the girl's face. Then he dragged long legs from under the tangled blankets and leaned over to feel on the floor for some socks.

He followed Annie out to the back door.

"Put yer boots on," he called. He was dressing as he

walked, pulling up overalls and stamping feet into workboots. He grabbed a couple of coats off a hook.

"And this," he added, tossing Annie's toward her. "Hang on, I'll do that . . . you'll have the door blown off its hinges."

"Well, hurry UP."

Annie waited while Old Joe lifted the latch, got a good hold on the door, and let it open. A wind hurled into the house, bringing a fresh seaweed smell and sweeping a calendar off the wall. Annie ducked out onto the verandah.

"DO YER COAT UP!" shouted Old Joe as he battled with the door. But the girl was gone.

She stood some way off, with her back to the wind— staring down at the first of the birds.

It was huddled between a pile of bricks and an old crab pot.

Wind tugged at its long feathers and the head hid under a sheltering wing. Annie bent to look closely. Beneath the ruffled feathers the bird's body was still. She reached out her hand, then changed her mind and nudged the creature gently with her boot.

Still it didn't move. Carefully, she pushed the crab pot away. The bird rolled slowly onto its side. Its head stayed under its wing and two big, webbed feet spread stiffly into the wind. Annie looked up.

The wind howled, low and lonely.

All around the yard, the birds were silent and still.

Then a cry came through the storm. Annie turned and saw Old Joe frowning, and rubbing at his hand. Close by, the body of a bird was slumped on the ground. But its head was lifted and turned toward Old Joe, pointing at him with a long beak.

"It's alive!" Annie ran over. "DID IT PECK YOU?"

The wind stole her words, but Old Joe looked up as she came close. Annie crouched down by the bird.

"CAREFUL!" Even beside her Old Joe had to shout over the gale. The bird sank its sleek head between hunched shoulders and stared up at him. The round eyes were like beads of polished amber.

"What'll we do?" Annie mouthed the words up at Old Joe. She pointed at the house, then back at the bird. Old Joe shook his head and gestured instead toward the boathouse. Then he shouted something and strode off in the opposite direction. Annie frowned.

"WHAAAAAT?" she called after him.

She got up, stamping cold feet, and scanned the yard. "There must be hundreds of them," she thought. Then she looked suddenly anxious. Perhaps most of them were dead.

The bird at her feet began to struggle into the wind—a few wavering steps—then stopped. The eyes closed, and the head hung down as if the weight of its own beak was almost too much. Annie looked up, her face strained with doubt. "Maybe they're all going to die?"

Old Joe was marching toward her. His hair blew out round his face and a scarf dragged out behind him. As he came he pulled on a pair of orange welding gloves.

"JUST THE THING!" he yelled, holding them up as he came close. Annie nodded. They looked thick and strong, and reached right up to his elbows.

Old Joe stretched out one gloved hand and poked at the bird's back. The creature turned its head wearily and opened its beak in a noiseless cry. The glove crept around one side and under its chest—then a second glove came down to clasp the other side—and the bird was held. It fought weakly to turn its beak on the gloves, and began to cry hoarsely.

Holding the bird at arm's length, Old Joe began to make his way across the yard. He kept a good watch on the bird's long beak, and on the vicious-looking claws on the ends of its feet.

"It's heavy," he grunted. He sniffed and twitched his nose, which had started to run. Annie hovered beside him, turning back and forth from the bird squawking in his hands to the others dotted about the yard. Several looked up as they passed, but most remained still, their heads hidden under their wings.

Old Joe followed Annie into the open end of the boathouse. They found themselves suddenly sheltered from the gale; a strange smell greeted them out of the gloom.

It took some moments to adjust to the dimness inside— and to see dark shapes amid the shadows. Then Old Joe walked farther in, and put down the bird. Annie followed him slowly.

The two gazed in silence at a mass of feathers, beaks and wings. Gray-feathered birds—the same as the ones outside— crowded the floor of Old Joe's boathouse.

"Well I'll be blowed." Old Joe's voice pierced the cushioned gloom.

"Shshsh!" said Annie.

Here and there a dark eye glittered or blinked—but not a head was turned.

# CHAPTER

# 3

OUT IN THE BOATYARD, ENDS OF COILED ROPE WHIPPED ABOUT like cut snakes and a stream of papers, bark and torn-off leaves swirled at knee height.

The girl battled through the storm—going from one bird to the next—bending down, looking closely, touching with hand or foot. "HERE'S ONE!" she would call out to her grandfather each time she found one alive. ". . . OVER HERE."

And Old Joe went to and fro, carrying the birds out of the storm, into the shelter of the boathouse. He worked hard, striding about the yard—with the big, orange welding gloves like gauntlets borrowed from an ancient king.

A few of the birds were strong enough to flap and scrabble away in fear. But most just dragged tired heads from under wings or lifted heavy beaks and pecked weakly.

Some of them seemed almost dead. By these Annie would falter, wondering whether to leave them and look instead for stronger ones, more likely to survive.

But then, in the midst of urgency, she would pause, strangely fascinated by the bodies of birds that were dead. The rigid bodies, caught in a stiffness that seemed somehow to be the very deadness of death itself. She would touch a leathery foot, or the cold bone of a beak—then snatch her hand quickly away. And there were other birds that appeared to be just as lifeless, but which flopped limply at her touch. Annie left them as dead, but was troubled by a creeping fear that they were just too weak to show that they were alive.

Old Joe paused in the entrance of the boathouse and looked out. "We'll have to go quicker than this," he thought.

The sky was no longer clear. Thick, dark clouds had gathered to the south, and behind the smell of storm-washed seaweed, there was rain.

The rest of the storm was on its way.

He looked about for Annie, then saw her coming from round the side of the verandah. His face brightened. "That's it!"

Trailing behind her was an old wooden billycart. It was a big one, properly made, with deep sides and four good wheels. The girl's face was red with cold, and tears ran from her wind-stung eyes.

"GO INSIDE!" Old Joe shouted, pointing. "IT'S TOO COLD."

"NO!" The girl shook her head.

Old Joe reached for the billycart rope. "GO ON!"

"I'm O.K.," shouted Annie, then, seeing more words coming, she turned away, safely deaf in the wind.

Old Joe kept a watch on the storm as he loaded the billy-cart with birds. He grabbed them quickly, and laid them inside while Annie pulled it along. The girl's fingers were cold and clumsy, and her ears ached from the wind. She held the rope over her shoulder, and leaned on it as the cart grew heavy.

Then, when there was no more room, Old Joe took over the rope and Annie followed him as he dragged the cart across the yard. A piece of loose roof iron began to rattle loudly in the gale. When he reached the boathouse, Old Joe stopped for a few moments and looked up.

"Gotta check the roof," he said when they got inside.

"Shshsh." Annie hushed him quickly.

He went on in a half-whisper. "Something loose up there." He picked up a ladder that was leaning against the wall. "Just hang on—won't be a tick," he said, and went back outside.

Annie stood watching the birds, struck by their proud stillness. Harsh, metal-scratching sounds came from the roof overhead.

"Come on, Grandad," she said to herself. She thought of the birds that were still outside—of rain coming and beating through their feathers. She began to search quickly for something she could use to lift the birds out of the cart. There were tins of paint, tool boxes, brushes, piles of wood, buckets of tar—and then, at last, an old potato bag.

Dragging it behind her, she went back to the cart. She bent down, and watched for a moment the small movement of a bird's shallow breathing.

"Hello, girl," she said in a low voice.

Reaching behind her, she felt about for the bag—then caught her breath in horror, and swung around snatching her hand away. She jumped up, and leaped back.

The bag was a seething mass of earwigs: waving feelers; long, brown bodies and pincers striking at the air.

Annie shuddered, thinking of them prickling down her back, crawling through her hair. Using a long oar, she pushed the festering bag far underneath the half-built boat and went back to the cart.

"Ugh!" she shuddered again.

A bird stared at her and blinked. Slowly she reached out a hand and touched the tiny feathers on the back of its head. The bird opened its beak a fraction. The hand froze for a moment—then moved on, lightly, over the smooth back.

"It's all right." The girl spoke softly as she stroked long and slow. The bird seemed calm and unafraid. Biting her tongue tensely, Annie closed both hands around its body. It didn't move as she tested its weight, then lifted it up.

A whisper of warmth came through the feathers. Against the dark gray, her hands looked thin and white.

Then suddenly, loudly, the bird squawked.

Annie gasped, and jumped back—dropping the bird head-first into the cart. Feet scrabbled and wings unfolded as it struggled to find a place.

Then angry cries gave way to silence.

And from all around the boathouse it seemed that birds were staring.

Annie pretended to examine her hand, and wished that the bird at least had pecked her.

Old Joe came in from the wind, rubbing and blowing on his hands. "What—you get pecked?" he asked, looking from Annie's face to the birds in the cart. "I said to wait."

"I was just trying to save time," Annie said. "Anyway . . . it didn't."

Old Joe grunted as he bent to lift the first bird out of the cart. "Was a good idea . . . rain's almost here . . . But you need gloves." He put the birds down side by side on the floor. "Tell you what . . . lucky thing I fixed that roof. You lose one sheet 'n' the wind gets in—next thing you've lost the lot."

When the cart was empty, the two went back outside. The air felt colder. The gale still blew from the southeast, but high clouds raced across the sky in the opposite direction.

"THAT'S THE CHANGE COMING!" Old Joe yelled, pointing up.

They filled the cart again and again, until—after the fifth run—it seemed that there were no more birds left alive.

But Annie searched carefully, tipping things over, or looking underneath—in case somewhere there was just one more bird, lying cold and exhausted but not dead.

Then the first raindrops came, driven in the wind, and in minutes the downpour began. Old Joe dragged the cart into the boathouse and took off his wet gloves. Outside, rain lashed the roof and wind screamed at the walls—yet in here, all was still.

The birds were gathered in silence.

They might have been statues—the work of an eccentric sculptor who carved the same bird over and over again.

# C H A P T E R

# 4

WET WOOD CRACKLED AND SPAT IN THE KITCHEN RANGE. OLD
Joe was bent over a big saucepan, stirring slowly with a long
spoon—and Annie stood beside him, turning pieces of toast.

"Don't know if this is breakfast or lunch," said Old Joe.
He turned to pour cupfuls of thick soup into bowls set out
on the draining board.

"Toast for breakfast—soup for lunch?" suggested Annie.

The two sat down on chairs pulled close to the stove.

"That's better," Old Joe sighed, and dunked some toast
into his soup.

"NOW tell me," said Annie. ". . . Grandad?"

"Give us a go," he answered through a mouthful of but-
tery toast. "—'n' you eat up too. There's plenty of time for
talking." He nodded toward the window—a patch of dark-

ened sky, rain beating against the glass. "Won't be doing much else while this keeps up."

Annie cut thin pieces off a block of cheese and dropped them into her soup, stirring them in with her spoon. They melted into long strings and wound between the steaming chunks of pumpkin, meat and potato.

"Well, they're muttonbirds, o' course," Old Joe began.

Annie looked up, surprised. "You mean the same ones we eat?"

"Ye-es," Old Joe answered, "but you only eat the young ones, out of the burrows—not these bigguns."

Each year they had a special barbecue, when a friend sent muttonbirds over from the island. Annie remembered the wonderful tender meat, the fat dripping down and hissing in the flames. She looked over to the window, frowning.

"Come on," said Old Joe sternly, looking at the girl's face. "It's food. It's like hunting rabbits, fishing . . ." He looked pointedly down at his soup and fished out some meat. "Or eating beef." The two sat in silence for a moment, listening to the rain drumming on the roof.

"Do you think they'll die—the ones in the boathouse?" Annie asked suddenly.

"Hard to say," said Old Joe. "Might. Or they might be all right after a rest—and then when the storm stops they'll take off again. Reckon it was worth a try, putting them in there." He smiled. "Don't know what they think of it though—they wouldn't be that used to indoor life!"

"What are they doing here?" Annie asked.

"Must've been blown off course by the storm, or lost their direction . . ." Old Joe paused, shaking his head. "Must be one hell of a storm to bring them down though. They're *sea* birds, used to storms." He settled back in his chair. "They'd have been heading for the islands—they turn up each year about now, for breeding. I've seen 'em, out in the Strait— thousands, millions of 'em—making a black path right across the sky." He made a sweeping arc with his arm. "Then sometimes they come down and rest on the sea—all sitting together, bobbing up and down on the waves. From the distance you think it's a huge raft or something." He paused to eat, sucking the hot soup carefully from the spoon. Annie took another piece of toast off the range.

"Where do they come from?" she asked.

"Well, when they've finished breeding, round about May, they head north—up past Japan, across a bit of Siberia, then down through Alaska. Heard of those places?"

Annie nodded. "I think so."

"Well, they keep flying until they come to a long chain of islands stretching out into the sea. The Aleutian Isles." The Aleutian Isles. Old Joe made the name sound like a mystery. "—Always wondered what kind of place that is. It's up toward the North Pole . . . I think there's Eskimos there, but I'm not sure. Anyway, that's the end of the voyage, one way."

"That's right across the world!" said Annie. "Just flying—with wings!"

"They probably rest on the water—with one eye out for sharks, I'd reckon! Anyway, they stay there for the summer, and when it gets colder again, they come back . . . round the other way—down past Canada and America, across the sea to Bass Strait . . . And," said Old Joe, almost proudly —as if it were his achievement, "back to the *same* island, and the same *burrow* as they nested in the year before."

"How do you know?" asked Annie.

"Used to read about all that kind of stuff," her grandfather replied.

Annie thought for a moment. "But how do the books know?"

"Dunno really," said Old Joe. "People study things, and write about them. They reckon they know." He laughed. "Maybe they don't." He picked up a pipe that lay under his chair and began to fill it with tobacco. "I'll tell you something my great-grandfather told me—that's your great-great-*great* grandfather. And this *is* true. It happened once when he was working on a ship that was looking for whales, somewhere down south of Tasmania." He opened the top of the range and poked a stick into the flames. He held it there until it caught alight, then pulled it out and used it to light his pipe.

"Yes?" said Annie impatiently.

"Well, one morning he went out onto the front deck of the ship, and saw this great big white bird. Just sitting there with its wings folded—and staring at him. He tried going up to it, and it didn't seem to mind at all (just as well 'cos it must have had a huge beak on it!) Then he noticed that there was something tied around its neck. So when he got right up to it—I don't know why the bird let him get so close, but it did—he untied it. It was a note, written in English, which said something like: 'Shipwreck. 3 survivors on small island.' Then it gave latitude and longitude measurements to say where it was, or pretty close, and 'Send help.' It was signed by the ship's captain and dated—er—the day and the month, some time in the 1860s. From the date, they worked out that the bird must have gone more than three thousand miles in twelve days."

"And what happened?" asked Annie.

"Well, it was too far for their kind of ship to go, so they headed back to Hobart, quick as they could, and reported it there. Great-grandfather heard that a ship was sent out, but never managed to find out if the men were found, or if they were dead or alive. Anyway, after they took the note, the bird just sat there—on the foredeck—for the whole day. Some of the men were a bit uneasy about it—thought it was watching them. Then, suddenly, out of the blue, it spread its wings and flew off. Great-grandfather said it must've been fifteen feet across, from the tip of one wing to the tip of the other, because it went up over the wheelhouse and its wings hung out each side . . ." Old Joe looked around. "That's as long as this room!" Annie's eyes narrowed in disbelief. "No —it's true. Would've been some kind of albatross—one of the big ones. Wandering Albatross, or a Royal. They get that big, but I've never seen one."

Old Joe got up and went over to the window.

Thin streams ran like veins across the yard outside. And down on the landing stage by the river, the storm-light shone through the rain—a yellow slab on a pole.

The wind raged on through the afternoon, rattling the doors and windows of the cottage, and driving rain across the yard in long, slanting lines.

Old Joe leaned his head close to a crackling radio, listening to the news.

"Nine-meter waves," he repeated. "Annie, what's that in feet?"

"Ummm—" she paused. "About thirty. Grandad how come you don't . . ."

"Shshsh! Listen."

The announcer went on to say that in a fishing port farther up the coast, boats had been torn from their moorings by a freak wave. Several of them had been lifted up more than five meters and dumped on the wharf—high and dry.

"Strike a light!" Old Joe shook his head, frowning. "It's certainly the worst storm in as long as I can remember. No wonder the birds couldn't cope."

"I'll go out and check on them," said Annie, getting up.

"Hang on a minute girl." He turned the radio down. "I don't know if that's a good idea."

"Why not? I'll only look."

"Yes but they need to be left alone," Old Joe replied. Annie looked disappointed and puzzled. "Serious. They'll be bothered enough being caught in there—'specially once they start to recover a bit. They'll want to get out, but won't be able to, coz of the storm. Last thing they need is to have a person in there, frightening them even more." His voice softened. "They're *wild* birds, Annie. Leave them be for now. If this keeps up we'll have to see about getting some fish for them tomorrow. Mind you—there'd be no boats going out in this . . ."

His voice was drowned by a sudden burst of hailstones pelting on the roof. Annie ran to the window. She watched the white balls bouncing on the ground and rolling away into dips and ditches; she saw them fall on still, sodden-feathered bodies. White spots on black.

The noise died down as the hail gave way to more rain.

"Grandad?" asked Annie. "Why were some of the dead birds stiff?"

"Erm . . ." Old Joe scratched his nose, thinking. "Well, it's because of—ah—all the muscles go stiff. Rigor mortis— that's what it's called."

"But some were floppy, and they were dead too."

"Yes—well, it doesn't happen straight away. You know, like when you pick up a rabbit you've shot. It's all limp, 'n' floppy. But if you left it for a few hours it'd be stiff." He searched the girl's face as he talked, but she seemed interested rather than upset. He went on. "Then again, if you left it even longer—not sure exactly how long—the stiffness'd go away."

"Is that when it's properly dead?" Annie asked after a few moments.

"No—it's dead—well, as soon as it's dead."

"When's that?"

"Well—erm—maybe when the heart stops—or the brain stops thinking. I don't know exactly."

There was a small silence; a boiling kettle hissed on the range. Then Annie spoke, "Is it the same for people?"

Old Joe sighed as he thought through an answer. "Yes.

When people die, their hearts stop—and all that. But it's not exactly the same. There's something different about people —and that means there's something different about when they die. And that'll do. Why don't you ask me something about boats?" He leaned over to pick up a piece of firewood, and then opened the door of the range. "Got any home-work?" he asked. Sparks flew up as he dropped the wood inside.

"Bit of math," answered Annie. "And I'm supposed to be finishing that project."

"Which one's that?"

"About Egypt. Remember?"

"Ah, yes." Old Joe pretended to look stern. "Well, I hope you're going to do some proper writing this time. We don't want another 'five out of ten—beautiful drawings, Annie, but where is the writing?' Do we?"

Annie laughed as she got up, stretching lazily. "It's all right, I got the writing done at school. There's only the pic-tures left." Old Joe looked thoughtful as he glanced around the room. "If you look on top of that chest, you should find a book—*Journey Through Africa*. It'll have something on Egypt. Might be a help to you . . ."

"Here?" asked Annie, beginning to sort through a crooked pile of dusty books and magazines. Old Joe nodded.

"Probably near the bottom," he said. "Haven't had it out for a while. Anyway you get on with that, and I'll have a think about some tea."

That night, Annie lay awake listening to the sounds of the storm, and thinking of the birds gathered safely inside the boathouse. She pictured them crowded together, sharing each other's warmth, waiting quietly for the storm to end.

And smiled to think of them there, on just the other side of the wall, inches away from her bed.

# CHAPTER 5

AWAY OUT TO SEA, THE WHITE BIRD BATTLED ON THROUGH THE storm. Pictures of lost hope circled through its mind: the silver fish; a brightening sky; a quiet sea. And fear. Muscles trembled with exhaustion and there was a buzzing in one ear. Where was the end of this storm?

And beneath pain and fear was the hard knowledge that this was the way of old age: stiffened joints and jerky movements; thinning feathers leaking air; fogged eyesight and bad judgment.

Sorrow and longing mixed with the memory of the bird as it once had been. Flying at its best in stormy winds like these, when nothing else could fly. Traveling for miles over empty skies in long, fluid glides, with scarcely a movement of the great wings. A good quarter of the planet had been home —since the time it first lunged from the cliff-top edge of the breeding island, throwing its life on the wind. And for fifty-eight more winters . . .

For just a moment, its thoughts wandered—and the bird was unready. Sudden turbulence came at the crucial point of turning near the end of a glide, close to the sea. One wing dropped sharply, the other flipped up, and the bird began to slip down through the air.

It sensed rather than saw the great wave towering behind, and scrambled in panic at the wind. Then turned, for an instant, and looked up—the dark eyes bright with fear.

The wave was a leaning wall of water, crumbling already at the top. It was too late to get away.

The bird dragged in a long draft of air and clamped shut its beak. It closed the great wings tightly about its body and tensed, ready.

The wave broke, grabbing the bird with rough hands, dragging it down. Salt water forced up the nostrils, feathers bent and broke and strong currents snared the wing tips.

Then the wave passed on, leaving the bird bobbing like wreckage on the sea. It stirred quickly, turning to face the wind—ready for takeoff. But another wave had followed the first one closely, and was already starting to break. The bird tried to swim across the trough, away from the tumbling foam. A desperate, useless race.

Again the bird went down—slammed beak-first into the dark water and rolling over and over. It managed to bring one wing safely against the body and was still trying to drag the other in when it pulled suddenly away. It twisted sharply back, sending a searing pain through the shoulder. The bird choked, breathing water as it gasped in agony.

Breaking the surface behind the wave, the bird looked down at the trailing wing. There was no blood. It tried to lift and stretch it out; there was a short, faulty movement, then nothing. Another try—panic overcoming pain. This time there was a nerve-jagging movement deep in the shoulder, and a sickening snap. The bird stared at the wing. There was pain and fear—and shock. The wing! The wing had never failed.

The crest of the next wave was drawing close. The bird forced itself to test the wing again. Painfully, but smoothly, it lifted up—as if something inside was back where it belonged. With the last of its strength, the bird managed a small run up the slope of the wave, spread the ragged wings into the wind —and lifted off as the first of a new wave reached for its toes.

# CHAPTER

# 6

IT WAS LONG AFTER MIDNIGHT WHEN ANNIE WOKE AND LAY still, listening into the night. Beneath the racket of the wind outside, an unknown sound wove through the dark—a low, nameless murmur.

The girl sat up, staring about, then leaned over and pressed her ear close to the wall. Her eyes widened. Through the thin, wooden boards she heard rustling, flapping and a myriad other small, feathery noises. Out in the boathouse, the birds were stirring. They called to one another—back and forth—in soft, gentle tones.

Annie dressed quickly, padded down the hall in her socks, then picked her way across the darkened kitchen to where her coat had been hung to dry by the range. The last embers still threw out heat and warmth folded around her as she put it on. Back in the hall, she stopped for some boots, then tiptoed quietly to the door.

She braced herself and opened it just a crack. A cold blast struck. She squeezed her way quickly outside, then leaned back hard on the door, forcing it shut.

The wind grabbed at her, ready to sweep her away, but she moved close to the wall, where there was some slight shelter from the gale. The yard was strangely light. Annie looked up as she edged along sideways. The clouds had passed away and a bright moon—almost full—hung still and calm in the wind-ravaged sky.

"Aagh!" She gasped suddenly as something caught at her hair, then ripped away. She spun around as it smashed against the wall close to her head—and fell. A broken branch, with long, dangling leaves like fingers. Her heart pounded. She went on past a corner and along a new wall— farther and farther—until she came, at last, to the entrance of the boathouse.

She walked around and stood for a moment, at the edge of the wind where the last wild shadows danced. Then stepped inside.

Birds called out as they shuffled and hopped; their noise covered her footsteps as she went farther in. The dark shapes were a milling crowd in the open space behind the half-built boat. A smell of sea and oil wafted from their feathers.

Annie came to some stacked crates, and crouched behind them, peering over the top. The birds moved awkwardly on big, webbed feet, tipping wings and touching beaks as they pushed their way around.

After a time, it seemed that some order crept into their movement. The shifting crowd began to center on a single shaft of moonlight that angled to the floor, cast in through a window high up the wall.

Bird noises died away.

Then all became still in the boathouse, though outside the wind raged on, tearing at the walls.

The birds stood wing to wing and beak to tail in a dense pack, around a pool of light that lay where the one shaft met the floor. As Annie watched, a movement spread through the crowd, a parting of the ranks—and a lone bird made its way to the light.

It stood there with its head bowed—a bigger bird than most, with long, sweeping feathers. Every beak was turned toward it, the ones closest glinting like knife blades as they caught the moonlight.

The bird raised its head.

"Aarchen . . . Ab . . . Aster . . ."

Annie stared in amazement as the sounds came through the dark. She watched the moving beak, straining to hear—but only short pieces carried above the noise of the storm.

"Berian bo . . . Crewan . . . Dessel . . ."

The girl crept closer to the gathering of birds and crouched again, behind a barrel of tar. The voice went on—the strange, meaningless sounds—each one cast separately into the crowd and followed by a short silence. "Faban . . . Farn . . . Hyer . . . Jed . . . Kat"—the voice faltered, and paused before going on—"my daughter Katera . . . Mowie . . . Nexus . . ."

Annie swallowed on a dry throat. "My daughter!" She stared, her face white and tense, her thoughts turning quickly. "My daughter Katera." Her lips parted and she leaned forward.

Something crashed against the roof outside and bounced its way down, gathering speed—bang, bang, bang-bang-bang. A ripple ran through the crowd as heads went down, beaks to the floor.

Then the voice went on, "—to those who have died here —and those long dead, the many generations of the Flight."

There was another pause, as beaks lifted. The bird in the light spoke again. "We must find the courage to turn from the dead. Rest has brought back our strength—and the Flight must be ready to go on. Exus the Bard will lift our spirits by telling from his Words."

A bird made its way to the front in small, hopping jerks—a strange movement which Annie understood when it reached the pool of light and she saw that it had only one full leg, the other being missing from below the knee.

The first bird left, and the Bard stood alone on the empty stage—a weird, one-legged shadow slanting away from him.

Once around the crowd he looked, and then began to speak.

*Does not the sun know when to go down?*
*And the dawn know its place?*
*Were the foundations of the earth not set?*
*And the laws of heaven and earth fixed?*
*The moon marks off the seasons.*
*Winter gives way to spring.*
*And the storm is followed by stillness.*

*For everything there is a right time—*
*To journey and to rest*
*To eat and to go hungry*
*To leave and to return.*
*There is a time for eggs to hatch*
*And a time for birds to die.*

*Let us turn from the dark of night*
*For there is joy in the dawn.*
*Warmth comes to the great land*
*And the sun follows her old footprints*
*Across the sky.*

The song of the sea is dear to us—
The gentle lapping against the shore
And the mighty roar of crashing waves.

We delight in the strength of the winds
That we may travel and not grow weary.
The stars hold true their places in the skies
That we may plot our journey.
The sun and the moon lend us their light
That we may behold the wonders of the great earth—
The jumping porpoise, and blue-flashing marlin
The spray fountains of giant whales
And gold-edged islands set in azure sea.

For we are birds of the Flight
And two homelands.

Bunjil the Eaglehawk watches over the Southland
The birthplace of our young.
And Binbeal the Rainbow, caught between sun and shower
Colors the skies where first we flew.
By rocky shores and wind-bent trees
Our burrows, our homes, are laid in the arms of the earth.

Five moons we stay,
Then Bellin-bellin the Crow empties the wind from his store-bags
To carry us north, over ocean wastes and foreign lands
Into the eye of the storm—and on
Until we reach our second home.

Raven Father watches over the North
A land still being made.
The earth rumbles and moves
Beneath its coat of green moss.

*And fire fountains blast*
*From white-topped mountain peaks.*

*Two moons we stay*
*Till summer leads us south again.*

*Dawn to day and dusk to night*
*High tide falls to low*
*North and South, through heat and ice*
*Our way is made—*
*A circle never ending.*

"So—" the Bard lifted his beak, "let us turn from the dark of night. For there is joy in the hope of dawn."

As these last words drifted into the darkness, a sound began—a single voice, soft but clear, floating above the endless wail of the wind.

The one voice was joined by another, then another—until the dark was filled with a wild and lonely song of many parts.

The call changed as it grew faster, lifting itself to a new note of triumph. Traveling, it seemed, beyond the wooden rafters and the roof, beyond even the turmoil of the storm. A song of hope lifting to the skies.

And then it stopped, with a suddenness that left the air trembling. Annie looked up, as if to watch the last echo rise, and disappear.

The first bird returned to the light.

"The Flight will leave as soon as the storm dies down—" he said. "Later tonight is my hope. If not, then we have no choice but to stay—and take our chances here."

A clamor of anxious voices rose: heads turned from side to side.

"—too close to the house."

"We're trapped in here."

"There's nothing to eat . . ."

"Where's the Weatherbird?"

"Where is she?"

"The Weatherbird! The Weatherbird! The Weatherbird!"
The calls grew loud and desperate—then died away as a ragged old bird shuffled slowly toward the crowd, from the boathouse entrance.

"All right—all right! Keep yer feathers on!" She spoke in a grating, crotchety voice, pausing often for effect. "As I have already said—this is *not* an—ordinary—storm. And—the keepers of the air—have not yet answered my call. Therefore—I can't be expected—to be *sure* what it'll do." She stopped, and drilled the crowd with hard eyes, challenging any thoughts of criticism. "But as I feel the wind—myself—it *seems* to be tiring. I'd give it a couple of hours. Maybe three." There was a flurry of relief, at which the Weatherbird tossed her proud old head and marched off again—as best she could on rickety legs. Then a voice called out over the chatter.

"Solar can't go. His wing won't work. It's not broken, but he can't move it."

Heads turned. "Where is he? Where is he?"

Birds standing close to the injured one stepped back—and he could be seen clearly, leaning up against a folded sailcloth not far away from the light. One wing hung down, brushing the floor with long feathers stuck out at odd angles.

Birds close by muttered in sympathy; others watched quietly. Then the first bird—the leader, Annie thought—spoke out. "How many others are badly injured?"

A soft rustling filled the air as a hundred wings unfolded. Then necks were twisted and legs stretched and bent—as birds examined cuts; bumps and swellings; damaged feathers; and torn muscles.

After a few minutes, the leader called for quiet. "Once we're off the coast," he said, "a group can rest at sea. And *every* bird that can *possibly* manage it, should do this." He glanced at Solar. "How many others *absolutely couldn't fly?*"

The crowd was silent.

"Then it's just you, Solar."

The injured bird stared down at the floor. "I'll have to stay," he said in a voice that was soft, but sharp with fear. "You'll have to leave me."

There was a solemn hush as the birds considered his plight. Then discussion broke out again: should he stay in here—or move outside to hide? What if there were animals around? What would he eat?

"The people—the man and the girl—they helped before," called a bird from somewhere near the back of the boathouse.

"Yeah," said another. "The girl dropped me on me head!"

Annie's eyes widened.

In spite of the strain, several birds laughed. But the leader bird was serious. "We can assume they'd probably help again, but . . ."

His voice broke off. Solar looked over to him standing in the light. "Well—there is always the danger . . ." The leader seemed reluctant to go on, but the birds were watching him, waiting. He looked away from the injured one as he spoke. ". . . that the girl'd want to keep you—as a kind of —play bird. And put you—in—a cage."

Cage? CAGE! The word grew, and filled the darkness. Horror fell like a blanket over the gathering of birds.

Annie bit her lip, watching tensely. "No," she thought. "I wouldn't—it's all right."

The injured bird stared about in panic.

"No, I wouldn't," said Annie, suddenly standing up. "You . . ." she faltered and stopped. She clutched at the side of the barrel. Hundreds of eyes stared at her out of the gloom. Birds close by shrank slowly away.

# C H A P T E R

# 7

ANNIE TOOK TWO CAUTIOUS STEPS TOWARD THE SHAFT OF
light. A path opened up ahead, the birds melting quickly out
of her way. All but one. A small, thin bird was left standing
just in front of her. Its narrow chest heaved as it stared up
with wide, fearful eyes. Alone in the empty space. Stranded.

"I wouldn't . . ." Annie began to speak gently, but at the
sound of her voice the bird broke into a wild flapping and
threw itself into the crowd, diving down to claw its way between the birds' legs. Fear spread out around it: wings beat at
the floor, raising dust; and feet scrabbled over heads and
shoulders as birds rode up over their neighbors, then fell,
beak-first, back onto the floor.

"I—won't—hurt—you." Annie forced the words out of
her dry throat. But no bird seemed to hear—or understand.

Feeling behind her for the barrel, she edged backward until her hand grasped the solid wood.

She stood there, watching helplessly as birds pushed against one another, tangling wings and hooking long beaks. Loose feathers drifted into the air.

Over in the light, the Bard held his beak steady but fidgeted with one wing and kept his eyes on the floor. Only the leader bird stood still and calm, looking out across the panicked crowd. The girl turned suddenly, and made for the boathouse entrance.

"I shouldn't be here . . ." she thought.

"Annie." A loud voice came after her. She spun around. "I have heard your name spoken. I am Tyde, leader of this Flight."

As he spoke, the commotion began to die down. "Our thanks to you—and the other. You saved the lives of many birds." He stopped, as if waiting for a reply. All but a few of the birds were now completely still, and listening.

"That's O.K.," Annie said hesitantly.

He turned his beak toward a space that was being cleared just to one side of the light.

Annie felt huge and clumsy as she picked her way back through the flock.

"Then will you also shelter this bird—Solar—until he is ready to fly on?" Tyde asked, when she was seated cross-legged on the floor.

"Oh—yes." Annie answered.

"—and promise not to detain him—in any kind of cage?"

"No—I mean yes. I won't."

"Then I put him in your care."

"But—what should I do with him?" asked Annie, looking anxiously at the hanging wing. "Once, my grandfather tied up a broken wing, against the body . . . Do you think . . . ?"

"You must do as you think best," said Tyde.

"Oh. Well—" She thought quickly. "What about food?"

"You needn't go to a lot of trouble there—bits of leftover fish—heads, tails, guts . . ."

"Flathead!" Solar, the injured bird, hissed through the side of his beak. "I like flathead. And . . ." he added hopefully, "crayfish?"

Annie nodded slowly, wondering how a bird could get a liking for something that lived at the bottom of the sea. She watched as Solar eased himself back against the sailcloth, and then turned again to Tyde.

The leader bird was watching her. His beak pointed to the side and one clear, bright eye held her in a steady gaze. The girl glanced awkwardly away, but was drawn back to look again into the deep, amber eye.

The beak opened, ready for speech.

But no words came.

Annie waited uneasily, feeling now the quiet scrutiny of the whole company of birds.

A gust of wind raced through the yard outside with a long, wild cry. But in here, the staring silence grew and grew—until the girl could almost doubt that birds had ever spoken.

Then Tyde stepped closer. He stood still and tall in the shaft of silver light.

"There have been others like you, who have crossed paths with birds," he spoke slowly and deliberately, as if his words had been weighed out and carefully chosen. "—Shipwrecked seamen; lighthouse keepers; lone yachtsmen; keepers of sanctuaries; and those who come to us, to learn about our ways . . . It has been the work of the Bards to gather knowledge from them, and to pass it on from Flight to Flight." The bird paused, listening for a moment to the wind—then went on. "Of course we have learned many things ourselves, by watching and listening. Then there are other birds . . . The seagulls, for example, have collected a whole network of information just by studying the things you have used and thrown aside—of which, I gather, there are plenty! But unfortunately not everything they say can be relied upon. So, we must take every chance to add to the knowledge of the Flight—and we would like you to answer some questions."

The girl looked surprised and slightly uncomfortable. What would she know? She fidgeted under the gaze of many eyes. It seemed some answer was expected.

"I can try." Her voice came out very small.

She looked nervously around the crowd as the Bard considered his first question.

"Are they all going to listen?" she asked Tyde. "What if I don't know?"

But the Bard had begun.

"Can you tell us why it is that lighthouses are becoming empty? The lights still shine, but there is no one inside."

"Oh," said Annie. ". . . I know about this from Grandad. They have automatic lights now. That means they work by themselves. They only have to be checked once in a while, so there's no need to have anyone living there."

"And what has happened to the keepers?" asked the Bard.

"Well, they must have had to find something else to do. Grandad reckons it's a bad thing, because as well as looking after the lights, they used to help in emergencies. Sometimes people's lives were saved because the keepers were there to see distress signals or bits of shipwrecks floating past . . ."

"We have heard of such incidents ourselves," said the Bard. "And they have helped birds as well. So *why* are the keepers being sent away?"

Annie shrugged. "To save money, I think."

There was a short pause.

"And who is this Money that the keepers must rescue?" asked the Bard. "Are they so important?"

"It's not a *person* they're saving," answered the girl. "It's *money*—you know, dollars and cents?" Tyde and the Bard looked at her blankly. "Well, it's hard to explain what it is . . ." Annie chewed nervously at the side of her thumb as she stopped to think. "Money is what we use to buy things we want. Like—if you had, say, a fish that I wanted, I could use money to buy it from you. Then it would be mine."

"So," the Bard said thoughtfully, "you could use the threat of this—money—to take away my fish?"

"No, it's not like that. You wouldn't *have* to give it to me unless you wanted to."

"But if I wanted to give you the fish, surely I'd give it to you anyway?"

"Yes, I suppose so," said Annie uncertainly. "But even if you *wanted* the fish, you might still rather give it to me, to get some money . . ."

"Ah—perhaps you can *eat* this money, instead of a fish?" suggested Tyde.

"No, it's made of metal—that's the coins—and the notes are just pieces of paper. It's not something you *use*, you just keep it and then give it to someone else if they have something you want . . ."

"But if you can't use this money, why would anyone take it in return for something real, like a fish?"

Annie sighed. "Just a minute. I'll try and work out how to explain it."

Tyde and the Bard turned away, and exchanged a few whispered words as they waited.

"I think," Annie said finally, "it's because we have to have a lot of things—to do with houses, food, clothes, cars . . . And we kind of swap things. One person grows food, or they're a fisherman, then another person might make things. My grandad builds boats. Sometimes people can just swap things, like we give potatoes to the lady in the shop and she gives us—" The girl stopped, suddenly embarrassed. "Well, she gives us—eggs. *Hen's* eggs . . ."

"Go on," said the Bard. "Where does the money come in?"

"Sometimes you have to use money because the other person doesn't want anything you've got. The man who sells gasoline—that's what we have to put in our cars to make them go—he won't take anything but money. And if Grandad made a boat for one of the fishermen, he couldn't get paid in fish, could he? We'd have whole roomfuls of them! So he'd get money instead, and he could use it to buy the things he needs."

"Yes, yes! I understand!" The Bard looked excitedly from Annie to Tyde and back—wavering a little on his one leg.

"So," the girl went on, "they have to pay money to lighthouse keepers—and that's why they changed to having automatic lights. You don't have to pay lights," she added unnecessarily. "So *that's* what I meant by saving money."

The Bard nodded his head slowly, then scratched himself thoughtfully with his beak before turning to the next question.

"We have heard people tell—but no bird has discovered what it is—of some creature called Yoo-eff-oh, that passes through the skies."

"Yoo-eff-oh?" Annie repeated, puzzled. "Oh, yes. It stands for Unidentified Flying Object . . ."

There was a hoot of laughter in the crowd.

"That'd be you, Silo!" called a cheeky voice.

"Shut up, Wal!"

The Bard ignored them, and Annie continued. "Well, that's what they call things when they don't know what they are—like they're not planes, or birds." The whole crowd seemed to lean forward as she spoke, every bird listening intently. "People say they come from outer space—other planets. Maybe other worlds like this . . ."

"Wahinagh," a bird said softly.

Tyde and the Bard looked at it sharply and it quickly hung its head in silence.

"What was that?" asked Annie. "Do you—know—about them?"

The Bard seemed to hesitate before making an answer. "We have knowledge of those who fly where no bird is allowed—in a farther part of the sky." Annie opened her mouth to ask another question, but the Bard went on. "I can say no more. Some things are not to be shared."

Annie frowned. *"You're* asking *me* anything you like," she thought, but she said nothing.

"Why are you making marks on your face?" asked Tyde. "Does it mean something?"

"I've seen it before," said a bird nearby. "They do that when they're angry."

"I'm not angry," Annie protested. "I'd just like to know . . ."

"Some things are not to be shared between kinds," repeated the Bard. He paused for a moment, then bowed slightly toward the girl, and moved back out of the light.

It was Tyde who spoke next. "While the storm is keeping us here," he said, "would you tell us a story?"

"A story?" Annie asked. "What about? I don't think I know . . ."

Birds shuffled in surprise and one or two repeated her words—"What about?"—"Don't know?"

"But you seemed to know a lot," said Tyde.

Annie thought quickly. A few stories came to mind—"Sleeping Beauty," "The Ugly Duckling"—but they seemed unsuitable. Then there was "Noah's Ark"—it had something about birds too—but how did it end?

"We don't tell stories. Not off by heart anyway." She grew suddenly irritated by all the whispers and nudging of wings. "Well, do you? And I don't mean the Bard—I mean all of you."

"Course!" a bird piped up from somewhere nearby. "Haven't you seen whole lots of birds sitting around together on rocks—or the sand? What do you think they're doing?"

"Well, anyway," said Tyde, "one of us can tell a story. Er—Tilla? How about you?"

Annie settled back against a tea chest as a new bird sauntered into the light and sat down.

"This is a true story," he began, "that happened once when I was crossing the Pacific. Somewhere between Cork Island and the 17th Rock, we ran into a very thick fog. It went on mile after mile, and I lost sight of all the other birds. Getting worried, I tried dropping down, to see if I could get out under the fog. Down I went—as far as I could without risking taking a bath—but the fog was still around me.

"Then suddenly, BANG! Just out of nowhere, I was knocked cold! I came to, with an aching head. The ground was moving underneath me, making a long, low hum, and there was a stale smell in the air.

"I called out softly, 'Anyone there?' No answer.

"Opening one eye slowly, I could see nothing but a hard, glinting white that didn't look as if it would let you through. Then I saw the sky—clear and blue—but trapped in a small round circle, inside the white.

"My head pounded and the noise droned on and on.

" 'A circle of sky,' I thought—and then it came to me. A window. White walls and ceiling, the sound that never stopped, the moving floor—a boat at sea. There I was lying in one of those brown cardboard boxes.

"Before I had time to think anymore, I heard a person walking. A door opened—more footsteps—and there was a kind of dressed-up sailor looking down at me. I was going to pretend to be asleep, but when he reached down into the box, I couldn't stop myself from pecking him.

" 'Well, well, little fella,' the sailor said. 'Bit better now, are we? There's someone wants to see you.'

"With that he picked up the box and carried me away through a door. Suddenly I could smell the sea and feel the wind—but then we were inside again. Here, it was quiet, with no stale smell. The sailor stopped to preen his clothes and hair. Then he went through *another* doorway—stood still for a moment—and bent over, holding the box out in front.

"I stood up, to get a look over the side.

"The whole room was full of the things people usually have in their houses. There were lots of chairs—of different sizes—a table, colored coverings on the floor, and pictures of people's heads stuck up along one wall. But the strangest thing was lots of flowering plants, cut off at the bottom of the stems and standing in holders of water!

"The sailor unbent himself and carried me farther into the room. Then I saw a woman sitting beside another table, with food set out in front of her. There were shiny cups, bowls, spoons, and a dozen *different* things to eat!

" 'Your Majesty,' the sailor said, 'here is the bird.'

" 'Bring it here,' she said.

"So there I was, in front of their Majesty—who I later found out was the leader. (She looked about half young and half old to me, but of course it's hard to tell with People.) The sailor told her how I'd crashed into the ship's funnel during the fog, and fallen unconscious to the deck.

" 'You're lucky to be alive!' she said to me—"

"Ay," came a call from somewhere among the listening birds, "that bit wasn't in the story last time!"

"It's TRUE!" the storyteller answered indignantly. "Anyway she invited me to share her piece of fish . . ."

The story was overtaken by the sudden noise of hailstones striking the roof. Tilla tried shouting a few words, then gave up and stood waiting for it to pass. But the noise grew louder, until finally Tilla shrugged his shoulders and went back into the crowd.

Birds huddled together, listening to the storm.

Annie wrapped her coat more closely and yawned into the dark. Outside it seemed some giant was at play—stirring up the winds, shaking the walls, and hurling stones by the handful from above.

# CHAPTER

# 8

IN A DAZE OF PAIN THE WHITE BIRD FLEW ON THROUGH THE night, dreading movement of its strained wing. Able to turn only to the right, by working with the left wing—and to glide, as before, but now rigid with anticipated pain.

It hardly noticed the passing of the hail, and the sky clearing—or the dark shadow that covered the sea ahead.

Then there were lights, a bright yellow sprinkling close together.

The long wings wobbled in the air as the bird faltered in surprise. Land! And houses, cars, roads—a settlement of people; the bird had seen lights like this before. Now, like then, it turned quickly away.

Sudden hope parted the cloud of pain. A little farther, and there would be rest, shelter from the storm. The bird battled up higher for a better lookout, and began to study the land below by the thin light of the moon.

There was a narrow headland that seemed to be covered with low grass, scattered with small dark shapes—probably trees. And up ahead was the dark ribbon of a river. It stretched from far inland, out to the rocky point, splitting the headland in two. On the river's edge, a little way from the sea, were several big, dark patches close together. Stands of ti-tree? Or an outcrop of rocks? Away from the lights of the settlement, it was the only promise of shelter on the open headland.

The bird dropped down and veered left across the path of the wind—an awkward turn, using the wrong wing. It fixed its eyes on a break in the line of dark shapes ahead and flew low, planning an approach to landing. Through the gap— then it would have to turn into the wind to land, in order to have enough control. Even so, judgment would be crucial. Too slow and the wings would stall—too much speed would end in a crash.

The longing for rest was mixed with concern. Since the old bird had chosen not to breed, there had been no need to come to any land—and more than three winters had passed since it had come down on anything harder than the giving, buoying sea. And now, it must land with an injured leg, a strained wing, and every muscle worn to its limit.

The dark shapes drew close, and the bird had to work both wings hard to hold a steady path into the gap. It shook its head as a sparkling mist gathered in its eyes—the dizziness of sudden pain on top of pain. It tilted the wings up, fanning out flight feathers, and spread and lowered its tail. Slowing down. The beak gritted against pain that came in waves. It let down its good leg like one wheel of a plane and pushed it forward.

Then—a sudden lurch of shock and fear. A light! Hidden by the shelter as the bird had approached from behind—it was seen only now.

And there were no trees or rocks—only straight, solid sides—all too big.

The light reached out, piercing, burning—half blinding one eye. Frantic wings launched a hard left turn, ignoring pain. Too far left—and straight in front, very close, was a high, dark wall. There was no room to turn again—and no time.

The bird leaned back its head and pushed its foot out higher, in a half-crazed hope of "landing" against the wall.

For a split second the bird pictured its end. The hard thud, then the body falling.

But at the moment of contact the blackness opened and took the bird inside.

# C H A P T E R

# 9

THE WEATHERBIRD SAW IT COMING AND SCREECHED A WARNING, a wild sound with no meaning—except that something was wrong, and was about to happen.

The giant bird invaded the boathouse—crash-landing and skidding along on its chest. The crowd scrambled, squawking in panic as the huge creature careened out of control. It thrust its hook-ended beak into the ground ahead, plowing a furrow, and scraping to a standstill just a beak length away from the mass of birds crammed against the back wall.

It slumped there with its sides heaving, and closed its eyes as if it neither knew nor cared what to do next.

Fresh blood appeared on one side of its head. It ran down the neck, beading on glossy feathers—red moving over white —and splashed on the dirt floor. Snowy feathers gleamed, reflecting the shaft of moonlight, but giving more back, as if adding a whiteness of their own.

There was a long moment of stillness as the gathering of birds—and Annie—gazed in astonishment. The albatross stayed where it came to rest. It leaned on its beak—a crutch for the tired head.

As time passed, whisperings began here and there, and more birds moved in, to stand grouped around the white bird.

Then every eye watched when—at last—it began to stir. Slowly, it drew in the long wings, bending one joint at a time, and folded them away. An aircraft dismantled.

Tyde stepped up to the bird. His dark head reached only just to the top of the rosy-yellow beak still planted in the ground. He began speaking in a low voice, the sound of the wind raging outside hiding his words from all but the one to whom he spoke. Once or twice the albatross responded, lifting the beak just a fraction and dropping it back. Then big, dark eyes half-opened as Tyde turned and motioned toward the girl.

Suddenly the eyes widened fully. The great head lifted itself up, holding the beak like a sword at the ready. A warrior bird—even now.

The head turned.

Annie started back in quick fear, as—forgetting its weakness—it lunged toward her.

Snap! went the huge beak. But at the second step, the bird overbalanced, sprawling helplessly on the ground. Quickly, it dragged itself up, and began struggling toward the boathouse entrance.

Tyde stepped in front of it.

"LISTEN." His urgent voice was bigger than his body. "This girl helped us. She and her grandfather brought many of us in here—to shelter. Without them . . ."

"You must be mad!" hissed the albatross.

A few birds shuffled in fright, but Tyde stood calmly, staring up the long beak.

"Brought you inside?" the albatross went on. "And why—do you think? Surely not for *your* good?"

Anxious whispers swept through the crowd; Annie felt many eyes turn to look at her.

"We have no reason to doubt it," said Tyde sternly. He spoke to his own birds as well as the white stranger.

"No reason! They're *People!* Isn't that enough? You—you of all birds ought to know . . ." The albatross paused, wincing at a twist of pain in its wing, then went on, slightly breathless. "I—have spent my life—wandering the seas—staying well away from them—and still I know . . ." It looked quickly back at Annie with a hard, ungiving eye. "There are warnings enough. One of the first stories I learned—about the betrayal of an albatross by . . ." More pain caused the bird to stop again.

"A mariner?" finished the Bard. He had hopped over to stand by Tyde, and somehow the two of them together seemed doubly small beside the white giant. Even Annie was dwarfed, as she crouched poised on her toes, ready to move —and darted quick glances to the boathouse entrance, measuring the distance that lay between. "I have heard that People tell this tale as well," the Bard went on. "They call it 'The Rime of the Ancient Mariner.' " He looked inquiringly at Annie.

The girl's face was blank, apart from fear. "Mariner? Ancient Mariner?"

"Sailor. A long time ago," explained the Bard. "Do you know the story?"

The white bird stood perfectly still—listening, waiting.

"Well, I do know a story," Annie answered cautiously, "—about an albatross. It's about my great, great, great grandfather—so it *was* a long time ago. And he *was* a sailor. The albatross came to his ship . . ."

"That's it," said the white bird, its voice hoarse with pain and exhaustion.

"Do you mean he was *your* ancestor?" asked the Bard.

In fear and confusion, Annie wanted to lie, but couldn't work out why. "Yes."

The albatross stared at her with mixed dread and fascination, as a diver would stare at a shark. Even Tyde looked shocked. She chewed anxiously at the side of her mouth as she ran through Old Joe's story in her mind. "I don't understand," she said, looking at Tyde. "What's so bad about it?"

"Khaaaaaaaaaaa!" The huge beak flew open as the albatross burst out in anger. For a moment the girl looked into the creature's dark throat—then leaped to her feet and jumped back. Her eyes turned to and fro, trying to pick out a pathway through the crowd.

"WAIT!" Tyde shouted. He flapped up to stand on a metal drum and faced the albatross almost eye to eye. "What happened back then has *nothing* to do with *her*. You can't hold it against her!" He looked up at the girl. The shaft of moonlight lit her frightened face, pale against the dark shadows of the night. He spoke to her gently. "Annie, you have proved yourself already—and won your own place in our storytelling. You need not be afraid. I give you the word of the Flight." As he finished speaking Tyde turned back to the white bird, and for a moment the two held each other's eyes.

There was a challenge, if not a threat.

The albatross was big, but the birds of the Flight were many.

Annie sat down again, a little way from the albatross. The two watched each other warily.

"Tell me the story," Annie spoke to Tyde without shifting her gaze. "I want to hear how you tell it."

Tyde listened briefly to the storm and glanced across to

the Weatherbird. "All right," he agreed, then turned to the Bard. "Make it a short telling—because as soon as we can, we must leave."

But the Bard was not yet ready. "Great-great-great-grand-father," he repeated thoughtfully, "I am unsure of what this means." He looked up at Annie. "Exactly how long ago did he live? We have carried the story of the albatross and the mariner since ancient times."

"Well, Grandad's pretty old," answered Annie. "And his father died before I was even born, so his *grand*father must've been dead for ages. Then there's two greats left, so —I don't know really . . ."

The Bard nodded. "Never mind, I shall tell you the story. Just as it has been kept and told by the many Bards before me."

"In ancient times a ship set sail," he began. "With a good wind and fair seas, it headed south until it reached the Line —or—" he looked at Annie, "as you may call it, the equator. But there it was struck by a fierce storm, and driven far across the sea, toward the South Pole.

"The air grew colder and colder; there was mist and snow. Mountains of ice, as high as the mast, came floating by. The ship was swept along between tall, snowy ice cliffs—like walls of emerald glass on either side.

"But then the ice closed up, ahead and behind. And the ship was trapped. The mariners were greatly afraid. In that land of ice and fog, no living thing was to be seen—unless it was the ice itself that screamed and howled as it cracked and moved.

"Then, from out of the fog came a great sea bird—an albatross. The mariners greeted it with much joy. They brought food from the galley and called the bird down—and though it had never eaten such things before, it accepted their offerings, and stayed among them.

"When it flew up again, it began to circle the ship. There was a thunderous noise, the ice ahead split apart, and the helmsman was able to steer the ship through to open sea. Almost immediately, a south wind sprang up, and blew the ship back northward, away from the fearful place of ice. And the albatross followed behind, flying down to eat or play, whenever it was called.

"Then—" the Bard paused, looking quickly at the albatross. There was a tense silence. "Then one of the mariners took a crossbow—and—shot the albatross . . .

"When his shipmates saw the bird fall to the deck, they cried out against the mariner, and all condemned him for killing the bird that had brought the wind and saved them from the prison of ice.

"Now there was no bird to follow behind, or to come down to eat or play. But the good south wind still blew and the ship sailed on. Soon, the last mists passed away, and the sun shone brightly in a clear sky. Then—and this is something we cannot understand—the shipmates changed their minds, and said that the *albatross* had brought the mist and fog. That the mariner was *right* to kill the bird!" The Bard stopped as hissing anger swept across the crowd. The white bird stood rigid. Annie's pale face was bent over, hands clasped tensely in her lap.

"The ship traveled on northward until it reached the Line —the equator. But there it was suddenly becalmed. The sea was flat—and still; heat and silence filled the air. Day after day the mariners waited for a wind to fill the sails of their ship. Soon there was no water left to drink, and in their thirst, the mariners were haunted by strange and terrifying dreams. It was not long before they began to blame their misfortune on the mariner who had shot the albatross. Their throats were so dry they could not speak, but they followed him with evil looks. Then they took the body of the great sea bird from the place where it lay on the deck, and hung it about the mariner's neck, as a sign of his guilt.

"But the winds did not return—at least not for a long time —and the story goes on to tell of the terrible consequences of the betrayal of the friendly albatross.

"The mariner and his shipmates suffered greatly.

"But—" the Bard turned to the girl, "—revenge cannot return the dead to life . . ."

# CHAPTER
# 1 0

THE BIRDS WATCHED ANNIE, AS IF WAITING FOR A JUDGMENT.

"That's not it," she said, "not the same as my grandfather's story *at all!*"

The albatross looked up in surprise, but with an edge of doubt in its eyes. The other birds nodded and whispered.

"And?" asked the Bard. "What else do you say about it?"

"Oh," said the girl. Her stomach churned in a way that reminded her of tests at school. "Well, it *is* a bad story . . . He shouldn't have killed the albatross." She fixed her eyes on a paint splash on the ground, and was quiet for a few moments. Then she went on, in a small, uncertain voice. "But people kill birds all the time—and eat them. Chickens, turkeys . . . geese, ducks . . ." She stopped. A barbecue every year—the hot fat dripping down, hissing in the flames —the tender meat. "Ducks—and . . ."

"And birds of our kind," Tyde finished for her.

Annie turned to him, with pleading eyes. "Yes! And me too—*I've* eaten muttonbirds. Not albatrosses," she added quickly, throwing a glance at the big, white bird. "But muttonbirds . . ." She forced herself on, to take her confession to its end. "Young ones—they take them from the burrows, before they can fly." Into the silence, the wind moaned long and low.

"We know this," said Tyde. He spoke in a slow, sad voice. "It has been happening for many generations now. In the beginning, birds waited and waited—out at sea—for the rest of the young to join the Flight. When they didn't come, storms or lack of food was blamed. Then, one year when it was time for the parent birds to leave, a few stayed behind—with the young—and saw what happened to them." There was a short, uneasy pause; then the leader bird went on. "We in our turn kill squid and fish, and eat them. There is this kind of killing, Annie—there is also murder, betrayal, as you have heard in the story of the albatross and the mariner."

"But how do you know which is which?" asked the girl. "If you tell me—"

"I cannot speak for you," said Tyde. "It's not for me to . . ."

"TA-YDE!" a loud grating cry cut through his words. It was the old Weatherbird. She stood on the top of an upturned dinghy and called across the crowd. "While others—sit around—telling stories—I—have been watching the storm." She unfolded one wing and carefully straightened some ruffled feathers with her beak. "The winds—are becoming weaker. Very soon—we can leave." Immediately, the birds began to jostle about, talking quickly in soft, excited voices. Tyde turned to Annie.

"We must be ready," he said. "But the albatross will need more rest before it is able to fly. I shall speak to it, before we

leave you together—but you must do your part . . . Help it
to trust you."

Annie nodded. "I'll try—but I don't know if it'll . . ."
Her voice trailed off as Tyde disappeared into the mass of
birds that moved all around them. Somewhere nearby Tilla's
voice carried above the chatter: "I hope it's not going to be
like last year. Got back to my burrow and found a *rabbit*
living in it!"

The girl followed the movement of the crowd, toward the
boathouse entrance. She saw Tyde standing beside the albatross; the white head was bowed to the floor, and his small
dark beak moved close to its ear. She kept a tactful distance
as she passed them by, and fixed her eyes on the square of
moonlight ahead.

A calm stillness covered the world outside.

Storm debris littered the boatyard. Trees held out tat-
tered, broken branches. And the still, dark bodies—the dead
of the Flight—lay scattered like fallen soldiers in a battlefield.

Annie began to search for the Bard, quickly scanning the
crowd until she caught sight of him hopping jerkily along
toward the river. She picked her way across and crouched
down beside him.

"Yes, Annie?"

"Oh—" She faltered, suddenly unsure of the right words.
"I just wondered—I mean I thought I should ask . . ." She
lowered her voice before going on. "What do you want me
to do with the—dead bodies?"

The Bard seemed surprised, at first, by her question.
"Whatever you like!" he answered. Then he seemed to recall
something. "Ah—that's right. You make a big thing of it—
with flowers, wooden boxes and special holes in the ground

. . . We are different, we place no store by a body without life, and usually leave the dead where they fall. But thank you for asking anyway. Have you seen Tyde?"

"He was inside, talking to the albatross," answered Annie, looking back into the boathouse. "No, wait. Here they come."

The leader bird glanced quickly around the yard and up at the sky as he came toward them. The albatross dragged itself along behind him, wincing in pain at each step.

"I think we'll have to take off from over there . . ." Tyde said as he came near. He pointed at the landing stage with his beak. "Now that the wind has dropped, it would help to have some height—especially for the birds that are injured."

Annie dragged over some of Old Joe's boat timbers. She laid them side by side over the steps to the landing stage, and made a ramp. The birds gathered around her in a tight pack —eager to begin the journey, to be back over the open sea. Looking forward to a good feed.

As soon as the girl stepped back, the birds began to work their way up the ramp. It was a slow and comic procession— they tripped over feet designed for swimming, and used wings as crutches to keep their balance.

"Annie," Tyde said suddenly, "I almost forgot. Solar asked if you would bring him out to see us go. He insists that if you hold him carefully his wing won't hurt too much. And —" he added reassuringly, "even if it does, he has promised not to peck . . ." The girl turned back toward the dimness of the boathouse. A sea breeze began to stir, bringing salt air in from the coast.

When she returned, cradling Solar rather nervously in her arms, the last few birds were struggling up the ramp. The albatross was slumped against one side—half collapsing, but unwilling to give in to sleep.

Tyde waited for the last of his birds to pass, then followed them up onto the landing stage.

There he stopped and turned back.

A dark shape. Silhouetted against a sky still soft with moonlight, but tinged with the promise of a rose-gray dawn.

He faced the girl, and spoke softly. "We shall carry your name to the sky. And far places. Remember us also."

"Farewell." He nodded first to Annie and Solar, then to the albatross. The light breeze quickened, ruffling his feathers as he walked away toward the rest of the birds.

Annie followed him, fixing her eyes on his dark head as he passed through the flock to stand at the end of the landing stage. He stood there for a moment with his wings outspread, then flapped quickly, lifting smoothly into the air.

A long cry floated back on the wind.

The air became a whispering cloud of moving feathers, beating wings—as the rest of the birds followed.

A black lace pattern spread against the sky.

Up and up they went—slender wings arcing through the air, in perfect fluid motion.

They passed across the face of the moon, one bird flying out in front, leading the way.

"I am Tyde, Leader of this Flight," Annie remembered his words. She pictured him guiding the birds through fierce winds, blinding fog and long nights of hidden danger. A tense frown marked her face.

The girl had stood here on the landing stage many times while Old Joe touched the prow of a new-built boat—sending it out to the unknown perils of the sea. There was a word he used that spoke of good travel and a safe coming home . . .

"Godspeed," whispered Annie.

The Flight left her far behind.

Tyde, the Bard, Tilla, the Weatherbird—were specks in the distance.

Then lost in the deep purple horizon.

They stood still in the warm light of dawn—the girl, the albatross and the bird with the injured wing. Alone beneath a wide and empty sky and the fading yellow moon.

# CHAPTER
# 11

SOLAR NESTLED DOWN IN A SOFT PILE OF WOOD SHAVINGS, while Annie gathered pieces of old, paint-stained carpet, to make up a bed for the albatross.

The white bird stood apart, in the middle of the empty floor. "I am an ancient bird." It began to speak slowly—half to itself, it seemed—in a hoarse voice that quavered with exhaustion. The girl stopped what she was doing, and turned to listen. "I have almost lived out my time. And that alone is the reason you find me here—an albatross brought to the ground. A few winters ago I would have played in winds like these . . ." There was a long silence—perfect stillness in a world without wind.

Annie watched the albatross, thoughts passing quickly over her anxious face.

"You could—stay," she said finally, in a hesitant voice. "Then when there's another storm you'll be safe, in here. I know lots of fishermen—I could get you any fish you like to eat . . ." As her words sank through the stupor of its tiredness, the albatross jerked up its head in surprise.

"Only if you want," the girl added quickly. "I just thought —perhaps—" she stopped to gather courage, "you're too— old—to be out at sea."

The great beak swung to the side as the albatross turned its head and looked at her.

"This is no place for me to stay—I am a bird of the skies and open sea. A time *will* come when the wind sweeps me from the sky and the ocean takes me into its depths. This is the way of things. But I am content. I have lived a long, long time . . ." The bird's eyes began to close, and the head sank down onto its chest. Annie bent down to finish piling up the pieces of carpet.

"You can sleep here if you like," she said softly. The white bird roused itself and struggled over, to crawl painfully onto the mound. It settled half leaning on one wing, with its injured leg sticking out sideways.

"Only an old bird gets bitten by a seal," it said, shifting around to make the leg more comfortable, "—or a stupid one."

The bird looked up with dark, sad eyes.

The girl searched awkwardly for words of comfort. "Grandad always says his hands ache in winter. He's old too. And some of his fingers are red and swollen all the time, from being hit too many times with a hammer . . ."

Smooth white feathers rose and fell, as the bird breathed deeply and evenly—sinking into sleep.

Annie watched for a while, then glanced quickly at Solar and turned to go.

Outside, the first rays of sun reached across the river, and lit the boatyard with a warm, pink glow.

# CHAPTER

# 1 2

IT WAS NEARLY LUNCHTIME WHEN OLD JOE CAME INTO ANNIE'S room.

"Rise and shine!" he said as he threw open the curtains. Sunlight filled the room and Annie stirred sleepily.

"You must have worn yourself out yesterday—to sleep in like this . . ." Old Joe went on. "The wind's dropped, and the birds have gone from the boathouse." The girl sat up, blinking in the sudden brightness. "All except for one little fella who's hurt his wing, and I've brought him inside, by the fire."

"What? Are you sure?" asked Annie, suddenly fully awake. "I mean you didn't see any other . . . ?" She looked quickly over to the window, as if hoping to catch a last glimpse of the great, white bird flying back out to sea. But nothing moved in the square of clear blue.

Old Joe looked slightly puzzled as he answered her. "No—I had a pretty good look. Just the one left. All the rest must've flown off." His voice softened. "I know you were looking forward to seeing them, Annie—but you should be glad they're gone. They'll be out over Bass Strait by now, heading for the islands—or maybe even down to Tasmania."

Annie nodded slowly. She looked at her clothes lying crumpled on the end of the bed—and saw the dust of the boathouse floor, and smudges of white droppings.

"That's the phone," Old Joe said suddenly. "Better get it." His voice trailed back as he left the room. "Could be some trouble, with that storm . . ."

Annie got out of bed and stood shivering on the bare linoleum. "It should've stayed and had a proper rest at least," she thought. "Could have waited to say good-bye . . ." She dressed quickly and went out into the hall.

Bright sun shone through the end window, falling in slanting shafts that were flecked with dust. Old Joe was hunched over the telephone, speaking loudly into the receiver. "Yeh. Yeh. O.K." He looked up briefly as the girl went past him, into the kitchen.

The kettle was steaming on the range. There was a new pile of firewood—just brought in, still wet.

And there, close to the warmth of the fire, was a white and gray bird nestled in a cardboard box of honey-colored wood shavings. Annie moved closer. White bandage criss-crossed over gray feathers—Old Joe had bound up the injured wing.

The bird's eyes were closed.

She crouched by the box.

"Solar?" she called softly, watching tensely as the bird stirred slowly, and opened its eyes. "It's me—Annie." The bird stared at her. No reply.

Annie leaned closer—searching the silent eye, the bead of silver brown. "Solar? Solar!"

"Terrible lot of damage," said Old Joe coming into the room. "Two boats lost. There'll be lots of mending needed doing . . ." He lowered his voice as he drew near to the girl and the bird. "The wing's not broken—just badly sprained, especially around this joint." He pointed to the middle of the bandage-covered wing. "There's been bleeding under the skin there. The thing'll be to keep him still as possible—then it should mend. But he'll be here for a bit. You better think of a name for him."

"He's got a name," said Annie. "He's called Solar."

"Solar? That's a good name. What made you think of it?"

"I didn't. *That's* his real name." Annie took a deep breath before going on. "I went out to the birds in the night, and they were—talking. And I talked back to them." Her eyes lit up as she spoke. "And there were different birds—Tyde, the leader, and the Bard—I had to tell them things . . ." Words tumbled on one another as she tried to say everything at once. Old Joe stared at her in quiet amazement. "Then an albatross came—a huge white bird . . ." The telephone began to ring again. Old Joe didn't move. Annie paused for a second, then went on over the ringing. "—Like the one you told me about. It crashed into the boathouse. Its wings were almost . . ."

She stopped talking as—with a quick movement of his hand—Old Joe reached into the top pocket of his overalls and drew out a single, long feather. He laid it on the palm of his rough, boat builder's hand. It gleamed softly—an echo of moonlight. A delicate curve of pearly white.

"Where was it?" Annie asked.

Old Joe swallowed as he answered. "Out there—in the boathouse. On top of some old bits of carpet. I . . ." His voice died away and he shook his head slowly. "And—what else happened?"

"I thought it would still be here." Annie stared down at the feather as she spoke. "It didn't like me at first, but . . .

I thought in the end it would've trusted me . . ." She looked up at her grandfather. "It should've stayed—I mean just until it had a proper rest. I was going to look after it."

Old Joe nodded slightly as he listened.

"Yes, but a bird's a bird," he said when she had finished. "As soon as it was able to fly—at all—it'd leave. Simple as that. Doesn't mean it didn't trust you to look after it."

Annie looked away, toward the window. Her bottom lip pushed her mouth into a grim line.

"Why don't you give it the benefit of the doubt?" said Old Joe. A crow flapped past, flying close to the window pane. A lazy raucous cry drifted out behind it.

As if in answer, Solar squawked loudly.

Annie turned back in surprise.

"Hungry, are ya?" said Old Joe to the bird. "You didn't happen to ask him what he likes to eat, did you, Annie?"

The girl smiled faintly. "Flathead. Or crayfish."

"Crayfish!" Old Joe laughed. "Fussy bird! Looks like we better sneak in a bit of fishing before they put me to work on these boats. How'd you like to pack up some lunch, while I phone Bill? Then we'll go out—and you can tell me about it all, properly."

Annie nodded, keeping her eyes fixed on the bird.

As Old Joe went back out to the hall, she leaned close to the small gray head.

"You don't *have* to have *fresh flathead,*" she whispered slyly. "Perhaps you'd prefer a tin of sardines? Would you?" Solar looked up at her. "Come on—yes or no?"

The beak opened, just a crack—then turned quickly and buried itself in soft, gray feathers.

# · AUTHOR'S NOTE ·

**The Wandering Albatross** is one of the largest flying birds. Ornithologists generally describe its wingspan as being up to thirteen feet, but there are anecdotal records of much larger birds. The Encyclopaedia Britannica (1937) quoted seventeen feet as the maximum measurement, from wing tip to wing tip.

A master of the winds, this albatross roams the southern oceans covering many thousands of miles each year. It travels alone, usually only coming to land for breeding. The birds pair for life and always return to the same nesting site, on one of the sub-Antarctic breeding islands. They have an unusually long lifespan; it is thought that some might live for more than eighty years. Most Wandering Albatrosses die at sea.

**The Short-tailed Shearwater** is best known for its spectacular annual migration. The birds travel in large flocks from one side of the Pacific Ocean to the other, and back, each year.

The Australian summer is spent on the breeding islands of Bass Strait (between Victoria and Tasmania)—each bird re-using the same nesting burrow season after season. In April/May the birds begin their long journey northward, probably driven by the need for food and to avoid the cold of winter. The northern hemisphere summer is spent at the Aleutian Islands, off Alaska, and in other parts of the North Pacific; then in August/September the birds head south again. These epic trans-Pacific flights leave the flocks exhausted, and vulnerable to bad weather and shortage of food. In some years large numbers of birds perish.

Commonly called the Tasmanian Muttonbird, the Short-tailed Shearwater is harvested commercially in Bass Strait.

---

**The "Words" of the Bard** are drawn from creation mythology belonging to the original human inhabitants of Southern Victoria (Australia) and the Aleutian Islands (Alaska). The Victorian Kulin told of Bunjil the Eaglehawk, Bellin-Bellin the Crow and Binbeal the Rainbow. Raven Father created the great land of the Aleutian Indians.

The Bard also borrows from oral poetry in the Old Testament.

**Tilla's story** is supported by numerous accounts of accidents involving birds and ships at sea. Some years ago, for example, a Great Shearwater crashed onto the deck of the *Queen Elizabeth*. A similar bird, disoriented in thick fog, flew into the funnel of R.M.S. *Caronia*—it was cared for by the crew and later taken to a bird sanctuary in Cornwall, where it recovered before returning to sea.

**Old Joe's story** has some points in common with an incident from maritime history: A Wandering Albatross, shot down off the coast of Chile in December 1847, carried a note in a small bottle tied around its neck. The contents of the note indicated that the bird had flown nearly 370 miles in twelve days.

**"The Rime of the Ancient Mariner"** was first written down by an Englishman, Samuel Coleridge, in the late eighteenth century. His version of the story is longer than that normally told by birds.

# ABOUT THE AUTHOR

Katherine Scholes grew up in East Africa, England, and Tasmania. For the last five years she has lived and worked in Melbourne—with story research taking her on journeys to Bass Strait islands, the Tasmanian wilderness, and Antarctica.

Her first book for children, *The Boy and the Whale*, was a nominee for the 1986 Australian Junior Book of the Year Award, and won for Best Children's Fiction in the 1986 Whitley Book Awards. Aside from writing, Katherine Scholes works as a film script editor and in film production.